The Necklace
and other stories

GUY DE MAUPASSANT

translated by
MARJORIE LAURIE

D1385771

A Phoenix Paperback

This translation first published in
Everyman's Library in 1934. Reissued 1991.

This collection first published in Great Britain in 1996 by Phoenix
A Division of Orion Books Ltd
Orion House, 5 Upper St Martin's Lane, London WC2H 9EA

Cover illustration: 'Empress Elizabeth of Bavaria in Hungarian
Costume,' by Georg Raab (1821–85), © Kunsthistorisches Museum,
Vienna/Bridgeman Art Library, London

A CIP catalogue record for this book is available from the British Library

ISBN 1 85799 609 7

Typeset by Deltatype Ltd, Ellesmere Port,
Cheshire
Printed and bound in Great Britain by
Clays Ltd, St Ives plc.

Contents

The Necklace
1

Mohammed-Fripouille
14

An Encounter
25

Mademoiselle Fifi
38

The Necklace

She was one of those pretty and charming girls who, by some freak of destiny, are born into families that have always held subordinate appointments. Possessing neither dowry nor expectations, she had no hope of meeting some man of wealth and distinction, who would understand her, fall in love with her, and wed her. So she consented to marry a small clerk in the Ministry of Public Instruction.

She dressed plainly, because she could not afford to be elegant, but she felt as unhappy as if she had married beneath her. Women are dependent on neither caste nor ancestry. With them, beauty, grace, and charm take the place of birth and breeding. In their case, natural delicacy, instinctive refinement, and adaptability constitute their claims to aristocracy and raise girls of the lower classes to an equality with the greatest of great ladies. She was eternally restive under the conviction that she had been born to enjoy every refinement and luxury. Depressed by her humble surroundings, the sordid walls of her dwelling, its worn furniture and shabby fabrics were a torment to her. Details which another woman of her class would scarcely have noticed, tortured her and filled her with resentment.

The sight of her little Breton maid-of-all-work roused in her forlorn repinings and frantic yearnings. She pictured to herself silent antechambers, upholstered with oriental tapestry, lighted by great bronze standard lamps, where two tall footmen in knee-breeches slumbered in huge arm-chairs, overcome by the oppressive heat from the stove. She dreamed of spacious drawing-rooms with hangings of antique silk, and beautiful tables laden with priceless ornaments: of fragrant and coquettish boudoirs, exquis-itely adapted for afternoon chats with intimate friends, men of note and distinction, whose attentions are coveted by every woman.

She would sit down to dinner at the round table, its cloth already three days old, while her husband, seated opposite to her, removed the lid from the soup tureen and exclaimed, '*Pot-au-feu!* How splendid! My favourite soup!' But her own thoughts were dallying with the idea of exquisite dinners and shining silver, in rooms whose tapestried walls were gay with antique figures and grotesque birds in fairy forests. She would dream of delicious dishes served on wonderful plate, of soft, whispered nothings, which evoke a sphinx-like smile, while one trifles with the pink flesh of a trout or the wing of a plump pullet.

She had no pretty gowns, no jewels, nothing – and yet she cared for nothing else. She felt that it was for such things as these that she had been born. What joy it would have given her to attract, to charm, to be envied by women, courted by men! She had a wealthy friend, who had been at school at the same convent, but after a time she refused to go and see her, because she suffered so acutely after each visit. She spent whole days in tears of grief, despair, and misery.

One evening her husband returned home in triumph with a large envelope in his hand.

'Here is something for you,' he cried.

Hastily she tore open the envelope and drew out a printed card with the following inscription:

'The Minister of Public Instruction and Madame Georges Ramponneau have the honour to request the company of Monsieur and Madame Loisel at an At Home at the Education Office on Monday, 18th January.'

Instead of being delighted as her husband had hoped, she flung the invitation irritably on the table, exclaiming:

'What good is that to me?'

'Why, my dear, I thought you would be pleased. You never go anywhere, and this is a really splendid chance for you. I had no end of trouble in getting it. Everybody is trying to get an invitation. It's very select, and only a few invitations are issued to the clerks. You will see all the officials there.'

She looked at him in exasperation, and exclaimed petulantly:

'What do you expect me to wear at a reception like that?'

He had not considered the matter, but he replied hesitatingly:

'Why, that dress you always wear to the theatre seems to me very nice indeed . . .'

He broke off. To his horror and consternation he saw that his wife was in tears. Two large drops were rolling slowly down her cheeks.

'What on earth is the matter?' he gasped.

With a violent effort she controlled her emotion, and drying her wet cheeks said in a calm voice:

'Nothing. Only I haven't a frock, and so I can't go to the reception. Give your invitation to some friend in your office, whose wife is better dressed than I am.'

He was greatly distressed.

'Let us talk it over, Mathilde. How much do you think a proper frock would cost, something quite simple that would come in useful for other occasions afterwards?'

She considered the matter for a few moments, busy with her calculations, and wondering how large a sum she might venture to name without shocking the little clerk's instincts of economy and provoking a prompt refusal.

'I hardly know,' she said at last, doubtfully, 'But I think I could manage with four hundred francs.'

He turned a little pale. She had named the exact sum that he had saved for buying a gun and treating himself to some Sunday shooting parties the following summer with some friends, who were going to shoot larks in the plain of Nanterre.

But he replied.

'Very well, I'll give you four hundred francs. But mind you buy a really handsome gown.'

*

The day of the party drew near. But although her gown was finished Madame Loisel seemed depressed and dissatisfied.

'What is the matter?' asked her husband one evening. 'You haven't been at all yourself the last three days.'

She answered: 'It vexes me to think that I haven't any jewellery to wear, not even a brooch. I shall feel like a perfect pauper. I would almost rather not go to the party.'

'You can wear some fresh flowers. They are very fashionable this year. For ten francs you can get two or three splendid roses.'

She was not convinced.

'No, there is nothing more humiliating than to have an air of poverty among a crowd of rich women.'

'How silly you are!' exclaimed her husband. 'Why don't you ask your friend, Madame Forestier, to lend you some jewellery. You know her quite well enough for that.'

She uttered a cry of joy.

'Yes, of course, it never occurred to me.'

The next day she paid her friend a visit and explained her predicament.

Madame Forestier went to her wardrobe, took out a large jewel case and placed it open before her friend.

'Help yourself, my dear,' she said.

Madame Loisel saw some bracelets, a pearl necklace, a Venetian cross exquisitely worked in gold and jewels. She tried on these ornaments in front of the mirror and hesitated, reluctant to take them off and give them back.

'Have you nothing else?' she kept asking.

'Oh, yes, look for yourself. I don't know what you would prefer.'

At length, she discovered a black satin case containing a superb diamond necklace, and her heart began to beat with frantic desire. With trembling hands she took it out, fastened it over her high-necked gown, and stood gazing at herself in rapture.

Then, in an agony of doubt, she said:

'Will you lend me this? I shouldn't want anything else.'

'Yes, certainly.'

She threw her arms round her friend's neck, kissed her effusively, and then fled with her treasure.

*

It was the night of the reception. Madame Loisel's triumph was complete. All smiles and graciousness, in her exquisite gown, she was the prettiest woman in the room. Her head was in a whirl of joy. All the men stared at her and inquired her name and begged for an introduction; all the junior staff asked her for waltzes. She even attracted the attention of the minister himself.

Carried away by her enjoyment, glorying in her beauty and her success, she threw herself ecstatically into the dance. She moved as in a beatific dream, wherein were mingled all the homage and admiration she had evoked, all the desires she had kindled, all that complete and perfect triumph, so dear to a woman's heart.

It was close on four before she could tear herself away.

Ever since midnight her husband had been dozing in a little, deserted drawing-room together with three other men whose wives were enjoying themselves immensely.

He threw her outdoor wraps round her shoulders, unpretentious, every-day garments, whose shabbiness contrasted strangely with the elegance of her ball dress. Conscious of the incongruity, she was eager to be gone, in order to escape the notice of the other women in their luxurious furs. Loisel tried to restrain her.

'Wait here while I fetch a cab. You will catch cold outside.'

But she would not listen to him and hurried down the staircase. They went out into the street, but there was no cab to be seen. They continued their search, vainly hailing drivers whom they caught sight of in the distance. Shivering with cold and in desperation they made their way towards the Seine. At last, on the quay, they found one of those old vehicles which are only seen in Paris after nightfall, as if ashamed to display their shabbiness by daylight.

The cab took them to their door in the Rue des Martyrs and they gloomily climbed the stairs to their dwelling. All was over for her. As for him, he was thinking that he would have to be in the office by ten o'clock.

She took off her wraps in front of the mirror, for the sake of one last glance at herself in all her glory. But suddenly she uttered a cry. The diamonds were no longer round her neck.

'What is the matter?' asked her husband, who was already half undressed.

She turned to him in horror. 'I . . . I've . . . lost Madame Forestier's necklace.'

He started in dismay. 'What? Lost the necklace? Impossible!'

They searched the pleats of the gown, the folds of the cloak, and all the pockets, but in vain.

'You are sure you had it on when you came away from the ball?'

'Yes, I remember feeling it in the lobby at the Education Office.'

'But if you had lost it in the street we should have heard it drop. It must be in the cab.'

'Yes. I expect it is. Did you take the number?'

'No. Did you?'

'No.'

They gazed at each other, utterly appalled. In the end Loisel put on his clothes again.

'I will go over the ground that we covered on foot and see if I cannot find it.'

He left the house. Lacking the strength to go to bed, unable to think, she collapsed into a chair and remained there in her evening gown, without a fire.

About seven o'clock her husband returned. He had not found the diamonds.

He applied to the police, advertised a reward in the newspapers, made inquiries of all the hackney cab offices; he visited every place that seemed to hold out a vestige of hope.

His wife waited all day long in the same distracted condition, overwhelmed by this appalling calamity.

Loisel returned home in the evening, pale and hollow-cheeked. His efforts had been in vain.

'You must write to your friend,' he said, 'and tell her that you have broken the catch of the necklace and that you are having it mended. That will give us time to think things over.'

She wrote a letter to his dictation.

*

After a week had elapsed, they gave up all hope. Loisel, who looked five years older, said:

'We must take steps to replace the dimaonds.'

On the following day they took the empty case to the jeweller whose name was inside the lid. He consulted his books.

'The necklace was not bought here, madam; I can only have supplied the case.'

They went from jeweller to jeweller, in an endeavour to find a necklace exactly like the one they had lost, comparing their recollections. Both of them were ill with grief and despair.

At last in a shop in the Palais-Royal they found a diamond necklace, which seemed to them exactly like the other. Its price was forty thousand francs. The jeweller agreed to sell it to them for thirty-six. They begged him not to dispose of it for three days, and they stipulated for the right to sell it back for thirty-four thousand francs, if the original necklace was found before the end of February.

Loisel had eighteen thousand fracs left to him by his father. The balance of the sum he proposed to borrow. He raised loans in all quarters, a thousand francs from one man, five hundred from another, five louis here, three louis there. He gave promissory notes, agreed to exorbitant terms, had dealings with usurers, and with all the money-lending hordes. He compromised his whole future, and had to risk his signature, hardly knowing if he would be able to honour it. Overwhelmed by the prospect of future suffering, the black misery which was about to come upon him, the physical privations and moral torments, he went to fetch the new necklace, and laid his thirty-six thousand francs down on the jeweller's counter.

When Madame Loisel brought back the necklace, Madame Forestier said reproachfully:

'You ought to have returned it sooner; I might have wanted to wear it.'

To Madame Loisel's relief she did not open the case. Supposing she had noticed the exchange, what would she have thought? What would she have said? Perhaps she would have taken her for a thief.

*

Madame Loisel now became acquainted with the horrors of extreme poverty. She made up her mind to it, and played her part heroically. This appalling debt had to be paid, and pay it she would. The maid was dismissed; the flat was given up, and they moved to a garret. She undertook all the rough household work and the odious duties of the kitchen. She washed up after meals and ruined her pink finger-nails scrubbing greasy dishes and saucepans. She washed the linen, the shirts, and the dusters, and hung them out on the line to dry. Every morning she carried down the sweepings to the street, and brought up the water, pausing for breath at each landing. Dressed like a working woman, she went with her basket on her arm to the greengrocer, the grocer, and the butcher, bargaining, wrangling, and fighting for every farthing.

Each month some of the promissory notes had to be redeemed, and others renewed, in order to gain time.

Her husband spent his evenings working at some trades-man's accounts, and at night he would often copy papers at five sous a page.

This existence went on for ten years.

At the end of that time they had paid off everything to the last penny, including the usurious rates, and the accumulations of interest.

Madame Loisel now looked an old woman. She had become the typical poor man's wife, rough, coarse, hardbitten. Her hair was neglected, her skirts hung awry, and her hands were red. Her voice was no longer gentle, and she washed down the floors vigorously. But now and then, when her husband was at the office, she would sit by the window and her thoughts would wander back to that far-away evening, the evening of her beauty and her triumph.

What would have been the end of it if she had not lost the necklace? Who could say? Who could say? How strange, how variable are the chances of life! How small a thing can serve to save or ruin you!

One Sunday she went for a stroll in the Champs-Élysées, for the sake of relaxation after the week's work, and she caught sight of a lady with a child. She recognized Madame Forestier, who looked as young, as pretty, and as attractive as ever. Madame Loisel felt a thrill of emotion. Should she speak to her? Why not? Now that the debt was paid, why should she not tell her the whole story? She went up to her.

'Good morning, Jeanne.'

Her friend did not recognize her and was surprised at being addressed so familiarly by this homely person.

'I am afraid I do not know you – you must have made a mistake,' she said hesitatingly.

'No. I am Mathilde Loisel.'

Her friend uttered a cry.

'Oh, my poor, dear Mathilde, how you have changed!'

'Yes, I have been through a hard time since I saw you last, no end of trouble, and all through you.'

'Through me? What do you mean?'

'You remember the diamond necklace you lent me to wear at the reception at the Education Office?'

'Yes. Well?'

'Well, I lost it.'

'I don't understand; you brought it back to me.'

'What I brought you back was another one, exactly like it. And for the last ten years we have been paying for it. You will understand that it was not an easy matter for people like us, who hadn't a penny. However, it's all over now. I can't tell you what a relief it is.'

Madame Forestier stopped dead.

'You mean to say that you bought a dimaond necklace to replace mine?'

'Yes. And you never noticed it? They were certainly very much alike.'

She smiled with ingenuous pride and satisfaction.

Madame Forestier seized both her hands in great distress.

'Oh, my poor, dear Mathilde! Why, mine was only imitation. At the most it was worth five hundred francs!'

Mohammed-Fripouille

'Shall we have coffee on the roof?' asked Captain Marret.

'By all means,' I replied, and he rose from his chair.

It was already dark in the hall, which derived its light solely from the inner courtyard, as is usual in Moorish houses. Over the lofty pointed windows creepers drooped down from the wide roof-terrace on which the warm summer evenings were spent. The table had been cleared, except for fruit of different kinds: enormous African varieties, grapes as big as plums, soft figs with purple pulp, yellow pears, long, plump bananas, and Tougourt dates in a basket of esparto grass. The mulatto who was waiting on us opened the door, and I went up the staircase, its azure walls bathed in the soft glow of sunset. I breathed a deep sigh of delight when I found myself on the terrace, which commanded a view of Algiers, the port, the roadstead, and the distant coasts.

Captain Marret's house, formerly an Arab dwelling, was situated in the centre of the old town, in the midst of those labyrinthine alleys which never cease to hum with the life and the strange population of the African coasts. Below us the flat rectangular roofs descended like giant steps, until they gave way to the sloping roofs of the European quarter. Beyond the latter appeared the masts of anchored ships, and beyond those again the sea, the open sea, reflecting the peaceful azure of the vault of heaven. We stretched ourselves on mats, with cushions behind our heads, and while I slowly sipped the fragrant coffee they make in those parts, I watched the stars as they came out one by one in the darkening sky. They were barely visible, so far and faint were they; they hardly seemed fully kindled. A mild warmth, delicate as the brushing of a bird's wing, caressed us, and sometimes, more ardent, less ethereal, from over the peaks of Atlas, came the breath of the desert, charged with the vague odour that speaks of Africa.

'What a country!' said Captain Marret, as he lay on his back. 'Life is sweet here. Repose has some special quality of exquisiteness. Such nights as this are made for dreaming.'

For my part, with lazy yet alert interest, drowsy, but happy, I continued to watch the stars flash out one by one.

'You might tell me something of your life in the south,' I suggested sleepily.

Marret was one of the oldest officers in our African army. He was a soldier of fortune, and it was to his trusty sword that he owed to his rise from the ranks. Thanks to him and his friends and connections, I had been enabled to enjoy a splendid tour in the desert, and I had come that evening to express my gratitude to him before I returned to France.

15

'What sort of a story would you like?' he asked. 'I have had many adventures during my twelve years in the desert, so many indeed that I can't remember a single one.'

'Tell me about the Arab women,' I rejoined.

He made no reply. Stretched at full length with his arms thrown back and his hands behind his head, he was smoking a cigar of which every now and then I caught a fragrant whiff. Its smoke floated straight upwards in the still night air.

Marret suddenly broke into a laugh.

'Very well. I'll tell you a curious incident that occurred about the time I first came to this country. In those days we had in our African army some extraordinary types, such as one never sees nowadays. They don't breed them any more. They would have interested you so much that you would have wanted to spend your whole life here.

'I was just a spahi, a young spahi of twenty, fair-haired, active and strong, a bit of a swaggerer, a regular Algerian swashbuckler. I was attached to the Boghar command. You know Boghar; it is called the balcony-window of the south. From the highest point of the fort, you have seen the beginning of that burning land, wasted, barren, grim, covered with red rocks. It is in truth the antechamber of the desert, the superb and blazing frontier of those vast regions of sandy solitudes.

'Well, at that time there were at Boghar about forty of us spahis, a company of the Bataillon d'Afrique, and a squadron of African light-horse. News was brought to us that the tribe of Ouled-Berghi had murdered an English traveller, who had come from God knows where, for all these English are possessed of a devil.

'This crime perpetrated on a European had to be avenged. But the officer in command was reluctant to send out a whole column, being of opinion that one Englishman hardly justified such a demonstration. As he was discussing the matter with his captain and lieutenant, one of our sergeant-majors, who was present, suddenly volunteered to punish the tribe himself, if he were given a squad of six men. In the outposts, as you are aware, the men enjoy greater freedom than in headquarters garrisons, and officers and common soldiers fraternize in a way that you do not find elsewhere.

' "You, my man?" laughed the captain.

' "Yes, sir. I'll bring back the whole tribe as prisoners if you like."

'The major, however, who was no slave to tradition, took him at his word.

' "You will start to-morrow morning with six men selected by yourself, and if you don't keep your word, look out for trouble."

'The sergeant smiled beneath his moustache.

' "Don't you be afraid, sir. The prisoners will be here by Wednesday at the latest."

'This sergeant-major, whom we called Mohammed-Fripouille, or Scallywag Mohammed, was a most surprising character. A pure-blooded Turk, he had enlisted in the

French army after a much chequered, and doubtless not very reputable, career. He had travelled in Greece, Asia Minor, Egypt, Palestine, and must have left a trail of misdeeds on his wanderings. He was a true bashi-bazouk, bold, fond of a spree, fierce, and at the same time merry, but with the placid mirth of the Oriental. He was enormously stout, but as active as a monkey and a superb horseman. He had the thickest and longest moustaches you ever saw; they suggested to my mind something between a crescent moon and a scimitar. His hatred of the Arabs was intense, and he treated them with cunning and frightful cruelty, continually thinking out for their benefit new stratagems and calculated acts of horrible treachery. To all this he added prodigious strength and courage.

' "Choose your men, my lad," said the major.

'I was one of those chosen. Mohammed believed in me, and by choosing me he bound me to him, body and soul. It gave me more pleasure than the *croix d'honneur*, which I won later.

'At dawn the next morning we set out, seven of us all told. My comrades were of the piratical, freebooter type, who plunder and roam in every land under the sun, and eventually enlist in some foreign legion or other. At that time our African army was full of these ruffians, first-rate soldiers, to be sure, but utterly unscrupulous. Mohammed had given each of us a dozen pieces of rope about a yard long to carry, and I, as the youngest and lightest, was entrusted besides with a single rope of a hundred yards.

When he was asked what he meant to do with all this tackle, he replied in his sly, quiet way:

' "We're going to fish for Arabs."

'And he gave a knowing wink, an accomplishment he had learnt from an old African trooper who hailed from Paris.

'With his head wrapped in the red turban which he always wore in the field, he rode at the head of our troop. Under his enormous moustaches lurked a smile of ecstatic enjoyment. And he looked really splendid, this burly Turk, with his powerful frame, colossal shoulders, and unruffled demeanour. He was riding a sturdy white charger of average height and seemed ten times too big for his mount.

'During our march along a rocky, treeless, and sandy defile, which unites later with the valley of the Chélif, we discussed our expedition in every accent under the sun, my comrades including a Spainard, two Greeks, an American, and two Frenchman. As for Mohammed, you never heard such a rolling of r's. The terrible southern sun, of which one has no conception north of the Mediterranean, beat down on our backs, and we advanced at a walk, as is the custom in that country. We marched all day without seeing either a tree or an Arab. About an hour after noon we halted by a little stream which trickled among the rocks. Then we opened our haversacks and ate our bread and dried mutton. After twenty minutes' rest we set out on our march again. By our leader's orders we took a circuitous route which brought us, about six o'clock, within sight of an encampment which lay behind an eminence. The low brown tents stood out like dark splashes on the yellow sand, as though huge mushrooms had sprouted up at the foot of this sun-baked hill.

'They were the very tribe we were seeking. Their horses were tethered a little distance away and were browsing at the edge of a stretch of dark esparto grass.

'Mohammed gave the order to charge, and we swept like a hurricane into the midst of the encampment. The terror-stricken women, their tattered white clothing fluttering around then, hurriedly crept and crawled into the shelter of the tents, and crouched there, uttering cries like hunted animals. The men, however, came running from all directions, eager to defend their camp. We rode straight for the principal tent, that of the aga. Following Mohammed's example, we kept our sabres in their scabbards. Our leader, as he galloped, was worthy of notice. He sat bolt upright in the saddle, as steady as a rock, while in spite of the weight it carried his little charger seemed as if possessed, its impet-uosity contrasting curiously with the imperturbability of its rider.

'The Arab chief emerged from his tent as we arrived in front of it. He was tall, lean, and dark, with shining eyes beneath arched eyebrows and prominent forehead.

' "What is your business?" he cried in Arabic.

'Mohammed checked his horse, and replied in the same tongue:

' "It was you who killed the English traveller?"

' "I am not answerable to you," retorted the aga emphatically.

'All around us a sound arose like the muttering of a storm. The Arabs ran up from all directions, and pressed close about us, vociferating furiously. With their prominent, hooked noses, their lean faces, and their ample robes flapping about them like wings, they resembled a flock of ferocious birds of prey. Mohammed, his turban awry, his eyes flashing, smiled, and his plump, lined, rather pendulous cheeks quivered with delight. In a voice of thunder, which quelled the surrounding clamour, he shouted:

' "Death to him who has dealt death."

'He pointed his revolver at the dark face of the aga, a puff of smoke issued from the barrel, and a red froth of blood and brains spurted from the chief's forehead. He fell backwards as though struck by a thunderbolt, and as he fell he flung his arms abroad and his wide burnous opened out on either side of him, like the pinions of a bird.

'I thought that certainly my last hour had come, so shocking was the uproar that broke out around us. Mohammed had drawn his sabre, and we followed his example. He whirled his sabre round him, driving back those who pressed too near.

' "Those who submit will be spared. Death to all who resist."

'He seized the nearest Arab in his herculean grasp, lifted him on to the saddle, tied his hands together, and roared to us to do as he did and cut down every man who resisted. 21

Within five minutes we had twenty Arabs bound firmly by the wrists. Then we pursued those who had run away. The crowd around us had fled headlong at the sight of our naked sabres. We brought in about thirty more of the men.

'The whole plain was covered with fleeing white figures. Dragging their children after them, the women scattered with shrill cries of terror. Yellow dogs, like jackals, circled around us, barking and showing their yellow fangs. Beside himself with glee, Mohammed leaped from his horse, and seizing the long rope which I had brought, he shouted:

' "Attention, my men! Two of you dismount."

'Then he did a thing which was both farcical and horrible. He made a string of prisoners, or rather a string of hanged men. Having fastened firmly the wrists of the first captive, he made a slip-knot round his neck with the same rope, which he then passed first round the wrists, and then round the neck of the next man. Very soon our fifty prisoners found themselves tied together in such a fashion that if one of them made the least movement to break away, he strangled not only himself, but his two neighbours. Their slightest motion tightened the slip-knot round their necks, and when they walked they had to keep the same step and the same distance from one another on pain of being brought down like noosed hares.

'When he had finished this extraordinary job, Mohammed began to laugh that silent laugh of his, which shook his whole body with noiseless mirth.

' "There's your Arab chain," said he.

'The rest of us were convulsed with amusement at the terrified and piteous faces of our prisoners.

' "And now," cried out leader, "fix a stake at each end, my lads."

'Accordingly a stake was fixed at each end of this string of captives, who looked like phantoms in their white robes. They stood as motionless as if they had been turned into stone.

' "Now to dinner," cried Mohammed.

'We lit a fire and roasted a sheep, which we tore to pieces with our fingers. Then we ate some dates and drank some milk, which we found in the tents, where we also picked up a few silver ornaments left behind by the fugitives.

'We were peacefully finishing our meal when I saw on the opposite slope a singular gathering consisting entirely of the women who had just escaped. They were coming towards us at a run. I pointed them out to Mohammed, who remarked with a smile:

' "That's our dessert."

'A queer sort of dessert it was.

'They charged madly down upon us, hurling volleys of stones at us without checking their advance, and we saw that they were armed with knives, tent stakes, and old cooking pots.

' "Mount," ordered Mohammed, and not a moment too soon. The attack was desperate. Their object was to sever the rope and free the prisoners. Realizing our danger, Mohammed furiously shouted to us to cut the women down. Not a man stirred. Seeing that we were taken aback by this new sort of warfare, and were hesitating to kill women, he charged our assailants single-handed.

'All alone he faced that tatterdemalion battalion of women, and the ruffian wielded his sabre with such insensate fury, with such mad rage, that at each stroke a white-robed figure sank to the earth. Such was the terror he inspired that the women fled in panic as swiftly as they had come, leaving behind them a dozen dead and wounded, whose blood stained their white garments red.

'Then, with face convulsed, Mohammed returned to us.

' "Let's be off, my lads, they are sure to come back."

'We beat a retreat at a slow walk, leading our captives, who were paralysed by the fear of strangulation. It was noon on the following day when we arrived at Boghar with our chain of half-hanged men. Only six of them had died on the way, but every jerk threatened to choke a dozen prisoners, and we had to keep loosening the knots all along the line.'

Captain Marret had finished his story. I made no remark. I thought what a strange country this was, in which such scenes could be witnessed, and I looked up into the dark sky and gazed upon the radiant phalanx of innumerable stars.

An Encounter

It was chance, the purest chance. On the evening of the princess's reception, every room in the house was thrown open, and the Baron d'Étraille, who was tired of standing, had entered a dim, empty bedchamber, opening off the brilliantly lighted drawing-rooms. Aware that his wife would not be ready to leave till daybreak, he was looking for an easy-chair where he could go to sleep. As he opened the door, he saw, in the middle of the spacious room, a wide bed with blue and gold hangings, suggesting a catafalque where love lay entombed, for the princess was no longer young. On the wall at the head of the bed, loomed a great patch of brightness, like a lake viewed from a lofty window. This was the princess's mirror, a trusty friend. It was festooned with dark draperies, which could be let down on occasion, but had often been drawn back. It appeared to be contemplating as a confederate the couch above which it hung. Round it seemed to hover memories and regrets, like ghosts of the dead that haunt old châteaux. The baron half expected to see, flitting across its smooth blank surface, exquisite reflections of rosy limbs, charming gestures of embracing arms.

Smiling and a little moved, the baron paused on the threshold of this bower of love. Suddenly in the depths of the mirror something stirred, as if the phantoms he had invoked were about to appear to him. He saw a man and a woman rise from their seat on a low divan, which was hidden in the gloom. As they stood there together, reflected in the gleaming crystal, their lips met in a farewell kiss. The baron recognized his wife and the Marquis de Cervigné. With all a strong man's self-control he turned and left the room. He waited till daybreak to escort the baroness home, but all desire for sleep had left him.

As soon as they were alone, he said to his wife:

'I happened to see you just now in the Princess de Raynes' bedroom. I need hardly explain myself further. I have no taste for recrimination and scenes, or for making myself ridiculous. To avoid all that sort of thing, we will quietly arrange to separate. My lawyers will regulate your position according to my instructions. When you are no longer under my roof you will be free to do as you please. But as you will still bear my name, I warn you that if your conduct gives rise to any scandal, I shall have to take severe measures.'

She attempted to reply, but he silenced her, bowed, and withdrew to his own room. He was hurt and surprised, rather than sad. In the early days of their married life, he had been very much in love with his wife. Gradually, however, his passion had cooled, and though he still had a mild liking for the baroness, he followed the dictates of his roaming fancy, whether in society or in the theatrical world. The baroness was very young, barely twenty-four, small, unusually fair, and thin – almost too thin. She was one of those little Parisian dolls, dainty, spoilt, exquisite, coquettish, sufficiently intelligent, possessing charm rather than beauty.

'My wife,' remarked the baron confidentially to his brother, 'is very sweet and seductive . . . but there's nothing of her. She's like a glass of champagne, all froth. What there is of it is delicious, but there isn't enough.'

Busy with painful thoughts, he paced up and down his room. At times a gust of anger swept over him, and he felt a savage longing to break the marquis's neck or to go up to him in the club and punch his head. Then he realized that it would be bad form, that the laugh would be against himself rather than his supplanter, and that, after all, his resentment arose from wounded vanity rather than a broken heart. He went to bed, though he did not sleep. A few days later all Paris knew that a separation, by mutual consent, had been arranged between the Baron and Baroness d'Étaille on grounds of incompatibility of temper. The matter gave rise neither to rumours, gossip, nor conjectures.

To avoid embarrassing meetings he travelled for a year, spent the following summer at the seaside, and the autumn shooting, and did not return to Paris till the winter. Not once did he see the baroness. He knew, however, that there was no gossip about her. She was evidently careful to observe the conventions, which was all he asked of her. Bored with Paris, he set off again on his travels. Then he spent two years restoring his country seat, the Château de Villebosc; after this he gave a series of house parties, which whiled away at least fifteen months. At least, weary of that tedious form of entertainment, he returned to his mansion in the Rue de Lille, exactly six years after his separation from his wife. Now, at forty-five, with a tendency to stoutness and not a few white hairs, he was visited by that peculiar melancholy which afflicts men, once handsome, courted, and adored, who feel their fascinations waning day by day.

A month after his return to Paris he caught a chill, as he emerged from his club, and developed a cough. The doctor ordered him to Nice for the rest of the winter. Accordingly, one Monday evening he caught the Riviera express. He cut it so fine that when he arrived at the station the train was already in motion. He threw himself into the first carriage he saw with a vacant seat. The far corner was already taken, but its occupant was so closely muffled in coats and furs that he could not make out so much as the sex of his fellow traveller, who seemed a mere bundle of wraps. At last he gave up the problem and settled down for the night. He put on his travelling cap, tucked his rugs round him, lay back and went to sleep. It was daybreak when he awoke. He again shot a glance at his companion, who had not stirred all night and who still seemed fast asleep.

Monsieur d'Étraille seized the opportunity to make a

hasty toilet. He brushed his hair and beard and did his best to efface the ravages which night inflicts upon the face of middle age.

'O glorious youth, how splendid are thy dawns!' quoth the poet.

Ah radiant youth, springing from its couch with glowing skin, bright eyes, hair shining with vital sap!

Ah melancholy awakening, when lack-lustre eyes, flushed, puffy cheeks, swollen lips, straggling hair and tangled beard invest the face with the drawn and weary aspect of age!

The baron opened his suit-case, took out his brush, and tried to make himself presentable. Then he waited.

The train whistled and came to a halt, which roused the baron's companion, who stirred a little. Presently the train went on. A slanting ray of sunshine penetrated into the carriage and glided across the sleeper, who moved again, and after a succession of little nods, like a chicken emerging from its shell, calmly unveiled and sat up. The mysterious traveller proved to be a woman, fair-haired, blooming, and remarkably pretty and plump.

The baron gazed at her in amazement. He could hardly believe his eyes. Really he could have sworn that it was . . . that it was his wife, but his wife so astonishingly altered . . . for the better. She had put on weight . . . quite as much as he himself . . . but in her case what an improvement it was!

She looked at him placidly as if she did not recognize him and calmly proceeded to lay aside her wraps. She had the poise of a woman who is sure of herself, the insolent complacency of one who awakes looking her best and freshest.

The baron lost his head completely.

Could it be his wife, or was it some other woman resembling her as closely as a sister? As it was six years since he had seen her, he might well be mistaken. She yawned, and he recognized her way of doing it. Again she turned to him and surveyed him with an expresion of calm indifference, without a hint of recognition. Then she looked out of the window. Bewildered, terribly perplexed, he kept stealing glances at her, while he stubbornly awaited developments.

Confound it! of course it was his wife! How could he doubt it? No two women had a nose like that.

A thousand memories stirred within him, memories of past caresses, of tiny details of her person. There was that beauty spot on her hip which was matched with another on her back. How often he had kissed them! The old sense of intoxication stole over him, as be recalled the fragrance of her skin, her smile when she threw her arms round his neck, the soft inflections of her voice, and all her coaxing ways. But what a change! What a wonderful change! It was she and yet not she. She had matured and developed. She was more feminine, more seductive, more desirable . . . more exquisitely desirable than ever.

Then this unknown, this mysterious woman, met by chance in a railway carriage, was his, legally his. He had only to say to her: 'Come!' Once he had slept in her arms, and her love had filled his life. Now he had found her again, changed almost beyond recognition. It was she herself, but at the same time it was someone quite different; someone who had budded, ripened, bloomed after he had left her; and yet, for all that, it was his old love still.

Her pose was more studied; her features were more marked; her gestures, her smiles, more sedate, less playful; nevertheless each trait was familiar. Two women were blended in one; the strange, new element mingling freely with the cherished memory. It was a curious sensation, thrilling, intoxicating, tinged with the mystery of love and with delicious confusion. It was his wife, reincarnated in a new form, in a new body, which his lips had never touched.

After all, he reflected, in six years the human frame undergoes a complete change. Only the contours of the figure remain and even they are subject to alteration. The blood in our veins, our hair, our skin – everything is renewed, replaced.

When two friends meet after long absence, each is confronted with an entirely different person, though he bears the same name and the same individuality. The heart itself may change. Ideas may be modified, principles altered, so that in a space of forty years, by processes, gradual but insistent, we may be transformed four or five times from one personality into another utterly new.

Thus he mused, stirred to the very soul. Suddenly there flashed upon him the memory of that evening when he had surprised her in the princess's bedroom. He felt no thrill of anger. She, whom he now beheld, was no longer the same woman, the same slight, fragile, vivacious doll of those distant days.

What should he do? How should he address her? And did she recognize him?

When the train halted again he rose from his seat and bowed to her.

'Berthe,' he began, 'is there anything you would like . . . anything I can bring you?'

She looked him up and down without a shade of surprise, embarrassment, or resentment in her glance.

'No thank you,' she said with calm indifference, 'nothing at all.'

He left the carriage and walked up and down the platform, actuated by an impulse to move his limbs and to pull himself together, as if after a fall. He deliberated as to what he should do. Transfer himself to another carriage? No, it would look like flight. Court her, pay her attention? No, she would think he was asking her pardon. Be masterful? No, he would only seem a brute, and besides, surely he had forfeited his rights. He returned to the carriage.

During his absence, she, too, had made a hasty toilet, and was now leaning back in her seat, radiant and serene. He turned to her.

'My dear Berthe,' he began, 'as Fate has brought us together again in this curious way after six years of a separation which was perfectly amicable, need we continue to glare at each other like a pair of mortal enemies? Here we are, for better or for worse, shut in together, *tête-à-tête*. Personally I don't propose to go away. Wouldn't it be pleasanter to chat like . . . like . . . friends . . . for the rest of the journey?'

'Just as you please,' she rejoined calmly.

He was at a loss how to continue. Then plucking up his courage he took the seat beside her.

'I see I shall have to pay court to you,' he said ingratiatingly. 'Very well. It will be a pleasure, for you are looking enchanting. You have no idea how wonderfully you have improved in the last six years. There's no woman to whom I owe such a thrill of delight as I felt just now when you slipped off your furs. Really I could never have believed such a change possible.'

'I can't say as much for you,' she replied without turning her head to look at him. 'You haven't worn at all well.'

'How unkind you are!' he replied, smiling ruefully and reddening.

'How so?' she asked, with a glance at him. 'I was merely stating a fact. Surely you're not thinking of making love to me. So what does it matter whether I admire you or not? But evidently it's a painfully subject. Let us talk of something else. What have you been doing all these years?'

'Why,' he faltered, completely out of countenance, 'I have spent my time travelling and hunting, and, as you see, growing old. And you?'

'Carrying out your orders and keeping up appearances,' she answered serenely.

An angry retort rushed to his lips, but he repressed it, and raising his wife's hand kissed it.

'I am very grateful to you,' he murmured.

She was taken aback. Really he was admirable; his self-control never failed him.

'As you were so kind as to respect my wishes suppose we talk now without any bitterness?'

'Bitterness?' she queried with a little gesture of disdain. 'I don't feel any bitterness. To me, you are the merest stranger. I was merely trying to put a little life into a difficult conversation.'

Fascinated by her, in spite of her cynical attitude, conscious of a savage, irresistible impulse to master her, he continued to gaze at her.

Fully aware that she had hurt him, she pursued relentlessly:

'How old are you now? I always thought you were younger than you seem to be.'

He turned pale.

'I'm forty-five,' he replied. Then he added: 'I haven't asked you for news of the Princess de Raynes. Do you still see her?'

She threw him a venomous glance.

'Yes, continually. She is quite well, thank you.'

Both of them stung to the quick, they sat side by side, their hearts in a tumult.

'My dear Berthe,' he suddenly exclaimed, 'I have changed my mind. You are my wife and I insist on your returning to my protection this very day. It seems to me that you have gained both in beauty and character, and I propose to take you back. I am your husband and I claim my rights.'

Thunderstruck she gazed into his eyes, seeking to read his thoughts. But his face was impassive, inscrutable, resolute.

'I am very sorry,' she replied, 'but I have other engagements.'

He smiled.

'That is unfortunate. I shall avail myself of the powers the law allows me.'

They were approaching Marseilles. The train whistled and slowed down. The baroness rose and calmly rolled up her wraps.

Then she turned to her husband.

'My dear Raymond, do not try to take advantage of a *tête-à-tête* which I myself manœuvred. In deference to your wish, I was merely taking certain precautions to safeguard myself against you and the world in general . . . just in case . . . You're going to Nice, are you not?'

'I shall go wherever you go.'

'I think not. If you will only listen to me, you will be perfectly ready to leave me in peace. In a few minutes you will see the Prince and Princess de Raynes and the Count and Countess Henriot, who will be at the station to meet me. I wanted them to see you and me together so as to convince them that we two spent the night alone together in

35

this compartment. Don't be alarmed. The two ladies will lose no time in spreading abroad this astonishing item of news. I told you just now that I had carried out your instructions and carefully observed the conventions. There was no question of anything else, was there? Well, in the interests of propriety I arranged this *tête-à-tête*. You particularly ordered me to avoid a scandal. Well, my dear Raymond, I have done so . . . You see . . . I am afraid . . . I am afraid . . .'

She paused till the train drew up. Then, as a troop of her friends rushed to the carriage door and opened it, she completed her phrase:

'I am afraid I'm going to have a child.'

The princess held out her arms to embrace her, but the baroness drew her attention to her husband, who was dumb with amazement and vainly endeavouring to arrive at the truth.

'Don't you recognize Raymond? He is certainly very much changed. He offered to escort me, so that I shouldn't have to travel by myself. Sometimes we indulge in these little escapades. For we're very good friends, although we can't live together. But this is where we part. He has had enough of me already.'

She held out her hand, which he clasped mechanically. Then she jumped down on to the platform into the midst of her friends, who had come to meet her.

Too much agitated to utter a single word, or to take any action, the baron slammed the door. He could hear his wife's voice, her merry laughter, as it died away in the distance.

He never saw her again.

Was she lying? Was she speaking the truth? He never knew.

Mademoiselle Fifi

The officer commanding the Prussian troops, Major Count von Falsberg, was finishing the perusal of his letters. He was lolling in the depths of a big, upholstered arm-chair with his boots on the fine marble mantelpiece, where, during his three months' occupation of the Château d'Uville, his spurs had worn two well-marked grooves, which grew a little deeper every day. Beside him on a marqueterie stand steamed a cup of coffee. The graceful little table was stained with liqueurs, burnt with cigar ends, and scored with the penknife of the conquering hero, who would pause now and then, as he sharpened a pencil, to scratch on its surface figures or drawings according to his idle fancy.

When he had read his letters, and had skimmed the pages of the German newspapers which the regimental postman had brought him, he rose from his chair, threw on to the fire three or four huge billets of green wood from the park, which these gentlemen were gradually denuding of trees to keep themselves warm, and went to the window. Rain was falling in torrents, the driving rain of Normandy, which seems as if hurled upon the earth by the hand of a madman, a dense curtain of water, a wall of slanting lines, rain that stings and splashes and drowns and is entirely characteristic of the surroundings of Rouen, that slop-pail of France.

The major stood gazing at the flooded lawns and the swollen Andelle, which was rising above its banks, and he drummed upon the window-panes a Rhineland waltz. A sound behind him made him turn his head, and he saw his second-in-command, Captain Baron von Kelweingstein.

The major was a broad-shouldered colossus with a long beard which spread out like a fan on his chest. His whole enormous person gave the idea of a peacock in uniform, a peacock which had its tail unfolded on its breast. He had mild, cold, blue eyes, and across one cheek ran a sabre cut, which he had received in the Austrian war. He had the reputation of being a good fellow and a gallant officer.

The captain was a short, red-faced man, with a large stomach, and was tightly laced. He had flaming red hair, and although he was closely shaven, the short shining bristles gave to his face in certain lights such a curious glitter that it looked as if his skin had been rubbed with phosphorus. A night of dissipation had, he could not remember precisely how, cost him two teeth, and this gap made him splutter when he spoke and rendered his utterance thick and difficult to understand. On the top of his head he had a bald patch like a tonsure, surrounded with a shining fleece of short curly golden hair.

The major shook hands with him, and then drank off his cup of coffee, the sixth since the morning, while his second-in-command made his daily report. Then they both turned to the window, and remarked that it was not very cheerful. The major was a quiet man with a wife at home, and adapted himself to circumstances. The captain, however, who was a man of pleasure, a frequenter of low haunts and an insatiable woman-hunter, chafed under the forced asceticism of a three months' confinement in this God-forsaken post.

There was a tap at the door.

'Come in,' cried the major, and an orderly, one of their military automata, appeared on the threshold, silently signifying by his presence that luncheon was ready.

In the dining-room three officers of lower rank were waiting for them. They were Lieutenant Otto von Grossling and two second lieutenants, Fritz Scheunauburg and the Marquis Wilhelm von Eyrik, a fair-haired arrogant little martinet, brutal to his men, harsh to the conquered, and as explosive as gun-powder.

Since his arrival in France his brother officers never called him anything but Mademoiselle Fifi. He owed this nickname to the studied elegance of his dress, his slim figure, which looked as if it were corseted, his pale face, which showed only a faint sign of a budding moustache, and his constant habit of expressing his sovereign contempt for people and things in general by the French expletive 'Fi, fi donc,' which he pronounced with a slight whistle.

The long dining-room of the Château d'Uville was an apartment of royal magnificence. But its crystal mirrors, starred with bullet marks, its long Flemish tapestries slashed with sabre cuts and hanging in tatters, bore witness to the diversions of Mademoiselle Fifi's idle hours. Three family portraits on the wall, a warrior in armour, a cardinal, and a president, were smoking long porcelain pipes, while in a gilded frame, tarnished with age, a noble lady in a tightly-laced bodice was wearing with a haughty air a pair of enormous moustaches done in charcoal.

Luncheon was a silent meal in this wreck of a room, rendered gloomier than ever by the rain. There was about it a depressing atmosphere of defeat, and the old parquet floor was now dingy as the earthen floor of a pot-house. After luncheon, over their tobacco and wine, the officers began to grumble as usual about the monotony of their existence. Brandy and liqueurs were passed round, and lolling back in their chairs they sipped glass after glass, without removing from their mouths the long bent pipe-stems with their egg-shaped china bowls, daubed with bright colours as if to captivate the eyes of Hottentots.

As soon as their glasses were empty they replenished them with a gesture of weary resignation. But Mademoiselle Fifi kept breaking glass after glass, and a soldier immediately substituted a new one. They sat lost in a haze of pungent smoke, sinking into that cheerless, lethargic drunkenness of men who having nothing else to do.

Suddenly the baron started up, seized by a violent revulsion.

'Good God!' he shouted. 'We can't go on like this. We

must think of something to do.'

'But what, sir?' asked Lieutenant Otto and Second-Lieutenant Fritz, both of whom had the heavy, solemn German cast of countenance.

The baron thought for a few moments.

'Why,' he presently replied, 'we will give a party, with the major's permission.'

The major removed his pipe from his mouth.

'What sort of a party?'

The baron drew his chair nearer.

'I'll make all the arrangements, sir. I'll send Old Faithful into Rouen to fetch some ladies. I know where to go for them. We will have a supper-party. We have all that's necessary, and at least we shall spend one festive evening.'

Count von Falsberg smiled and shrugged his shoulders:

'You must be crazy, my dear fellow.'

But all the other officers sprang from their chairs and surrounded the major.

'Don't say no, sir,' they pleaded. 'It's so deadly dull here.'

At last the major gave in. The baron sent for Old Faithful, a non-commissioned officer of long service, who had never been known to smile and who carried out with fanatical devotion all his officer's orders, no matter what they were.

Impassive as ever, Old Faithful received the baron's instructions. He left the room, and five minutes later a huge commissariat cart with a hood over it set off through the driving rain, drawn by four horses at a gallop. Immediately an awakening thrill seemed to stir the pulses of all the officers. They roused themselves from their languid postures; their faces brightened and they began to talk. Although the rain was pouring down with all its former violence, the major observed that it was not so dark, and Lieutenant Otto declared with conviction that it was going to clear up. Mademoiselle Fifi seemed unable to keep still. He was for ever jumping up and sitting down again. His hard, keen eyes scanned the room, looking for something to destroy. Suddenly the young reprobate fixed his gaze on the lady with the moustaches and drew his revolver.

'At any rate you shan't see it,' he exclaimed, and without rising from his chair he took aim. With two successive shots he pierced both her eyes.

'And now we'll have a mine,' he cried.

At this conversation ceased at once, as if a new and absorbing interest had presented itself. Springing mines was Mademoiselle Fifi's own invention, his own patent method of destruction and his favourite pastime. The rightful owner, Count Fernand d'Anoys d'Uville, had had to abandon the château so hastily that he had had no time to remove or hide any of his treasures, with the exception of the silver, which he concealed in a hole in the wall. He was a man of great wealth and magnificent tastes. Before his headlong flight, his great drawing-room, which opened off the dining-hall, had presented the aspect of a gallery in a museum. The walls were hung with oil paintings, drawings, and valuable water-colours. Tables, stands, and elegant class cases displayed a thousand oranments, vases of

Japanese porcelain, statuettes, Chinese grotesques, ivory antiques, Venetian glass, so that the spacious apartment seemed thronged by a multitude of fantastic and precious denizens. Scarce one had survived. It was not that there had been any looting; this the major would never have permitted. But now and then Mademoiselle Fifi would spring a mine, and on these occasions all the officers really enjoyed themselves for quite five minutes.

The young marquis strolled into the drawing-room to look for what he required. He returned with an exquisite little teapot of *famille rose*. This he filled with gunpowder, and through the spout he carefully inserted a long fuse, which he lighted. Then he ran back to the drawing-room to deposit his infernal machine. He returned hastily to the dining-room and closed the door behind him. The German officers stood waiting with a smile of childish expectation on their faces, and as soon as the explosion had reverberated through the château they made a rush for the drawing-room. Mademoiselle Fifi was the first to enter. He clapped his hands in wild delight over a Venus in terra-cotta with its head blown off at last. His companions picked up fragments of procelain, admiring the curious denticulations produced by the explosion, examined the fresh damage and debated whether this wreckage and that had not been caused by a previous mine. The major cast a benevolent glance around the great drawing-room, ruined in this Nero-like fashion, and strewn with shattered treasures of art. As he led the way out he remarked genially:

'That was a very successful effort.'

The atmosphere in the dining-room was so thick with mingled fumes of gunpowder and tobacco that it was impossible to breathe. The major threw open the window, and all the officers, who had come back for a final glass of brandy, gathered around it. The damp air rushed into the room in a fine spray which clung to their beards and moustaches and diffused a smell of sodden earth. They looked out at the tall trees, bowed beneath the deluge; at the wide valley shrouded in mists emanating from the water that poured from the low black clouds; at the distant belfry of the church, rising through the driving rain like a grey spike.

The church bell had never been rung since the first day of their occupation. The silence of this belfry, however, was the only form of resistance that the invaders had encountered throughout the district. The parish priest had in no way declined to receive or entertain the Prussian soldiers. On several occasions he had even gone so far as to drink a bottle of beer or Bordeaux with the Prussian commandant, who often employed him as a benevolent intermediary. But it was useless to ask him for even a single tinkle of his bell. He would have been shot rather than yield. This was his own special form of protest against the invasion; a pacific, a silent protest, the only protest, the only protest proper for a priest, a man of peace and not a man of blood. For ten miles round every one praised the firmness and heroism of the Abbé Chantavoine, who dared to assert and proclaim the public mourning by the persistent silence of his belfry. Inspired by his example, the whole village was prepared to support its pastor to the utmost, and to dare the worst, deeming this tacit protest a safeguard of the national honour. It seemed to the peasants that they deserved better of their country than either Belfort or Strasbourg; that they had set as fine an example, and had won immortal honour for their hamlet. With this one reservation, they refused the Prussian conquerors nothing. The major and his officers laughed together over this exhibition of harmless bravado, and as the whole village showed itself deferential and obliging towards the conquerors, they willingly tolerated this mute display of patriotism.

Only the young Marquis Wilhelm wanted to insist upon the bell being rung. The diplomatic condescension with which his superior officer treated the priest infuriated him, and every day he besought the major to order a single ding-dong, just once, once only, for fun. He pleaded with the coaxing grace of a cat, the winning wiles of a woman, the wheedling tones of a mistress who has set her heart on something. But the major would not give in, and Mademoiselle Fifi had to console himself with springing mines in the Château d'Uville.

For several minutes the five men remained grouped at the window, breathing the damp air. At last Lieutenant Fritz said with a husky laugh:

'I'm afraid those ladies won't have good weather for their drive.'

Then they dispersed. Each man went off to his work; the captain, for his part, had a great many preparations to make for the supper-party.

Towards evening they met again, and they burst out laughing when they saw how spick and span they all were, each one of them as carefully perfumed and pomaded as if for a grand review. The major's hair looked a shade less grey than in the morning. The captain had shaved and had retained only his moustache, which lay like a line of flame on his upper lip. One or other of them kept going to the window, which had been left open in spite of the rain. At ten minutes past six the baron announced that he heard a rumble of wheels in the distance. They all rushed to the door, and soon the heavy vehicle arrived at the château at a gallop, its four horses steaming and panting and splashed with mud up to the withers.

Five young women alighted on the perron, five handsome girls, carefully selected by a brother officer, to whom Old Faithful had delivered a note from the captain. They had raised no objections. They were sure of being well paid, and thanks to their experiences of the last three months, they were used to Prussians. Philosophically they accepted men and things as they came.

'It's all in the day's work,' they remarked during the drive, as if to quiet the secret qualms of such vestiges of conscience as still remained to them.

They were ushered at once into the dining-room. When it was lighted up it seemed drearier than ever in its pitiful condition of dilapidation. The table, laden with food, exquisite china, and the silver that had been unearthed from its hiding-place in the wall, gave it the appearance of a tavern full of bandits, supping after a successful raid. Wreathed in smiles, the captain took possession of the ladies, viewing them with the air of an expert, kissing them, breathing in their perfume and estimating them at their professional value. The junior officers were eager to appropriate a lady apiece, but he refused to allow this, authoritatively claimng the right to distribute the young women with due respect for rank and seniority. In order to avoid all arguments, disputes, and accusations of partiality he ranged the five girls in a row according to height. Addressing the tallest one, he said in a voice of command:

'Your name?'

'Paméla, she replied in soldierly tones.

'Number one, name of Paméla, awarded to the major.'

Then the captain kissed Blondine, the next in height, in token of ownership. Buxon Amanda was assigned to Lieutenant Otto; Éva the Tomato to Second Lieutenant Fritz; and to slim Wilhelm von Eyrik, the most junior of the officers, Rachel, the smallest girl, a young brunette with eyes as black as ink, a Jewess, whose turned-up nose served to prove the rule which attributes hooked noses to all her race. They were all sufficiently pretty and plump, with nothing particularly distinctive in their faces. In figure and complexion all conformed more or less to the same type, by virtue of their daily traffic and their common existence in houses of resort.

The three junior officers were anxious to carry off their young women at once on the pretext of lending them hair-brushes and soap. But the captain very sensibly objected to this proposal. He declared that the ladies were quite tidy enough for dinner, and that if they took their partners to their rooms now they would only want to change them when they came down again, and would interfere with the other couples. They accepted the expert's advice and contented themselves with innumerable kisses by way of a preliminary. All at once Rachel began to choke; she coughed till the tears came into her eyes, while smoke issued from her nostrils. Pretending that he wanted to kiss her, the marquis had puffed tobacco smoke into her mouth. She did not fly into a rage, or utter a single reproach. She merely gazed fixedly at her owner with dawning anger in the depths of her dark eyes.

They sat down to dinner. Even the major appeared to be enjoying himself. He placed Paméla on his right and Blondine on his left, remarking as he unfolded his table-napkin:

'It was certainly an excellent idea of yours, captain.'

Lieutenant Otto and Lieutenant Fritz were as polite as if in the company of women of their own class, somewhat to the embarrassment of their neighbours. But Baron von Kelweingstein, radiant and revelling in his favourite vice, kept making unseemly jokes, while his halo of red hair appeared to blaze. He made love in his Rhenish French, expectorating his tap-room gallantries through the gap left by his two broken teeth. The women, however, could not understand him. They gave no sign of intelligence except when he spluttered out obscene words and gross expressions, which were mangled by his accent. At this they all went off into wild shrieks of laughter, falling on their neighbours' necks and mimicking the baron, who kept purposely mispronouncing his words for the pleasure of hearing them repeat his coarse phrases. The first few bottles of wine had gone to the young women's heads. They poured out a flow of vile language and, once more their natural selves, they resumed all their usual habits, lavishing kisses right and left, pinching their neighbours' arms, uttering shrill cries, and drinking out of anybody's glass. Now and then one of them would shout a verse or two of French, or a snatch of a German song picked up during her daily intercourse with the enemy.

Before very long, intoxicated with all this femininity within their reach, the men, too, lost their heads. They shouted and broke the plates, while behind their chairs the orderlies waited on them impassively. The major alone preserved some degree of self-control.

Mademoiselle Fifi had taken Rachel on his knees. Sometimes in a gust of frigid passion he frantically kissed the ebony ringlets on her neck, and breathed in the warmth and fragrance of her person. Sometimes with savage ferocity he pinched her so violently through her dress that he made her cry out. Again, crushing her in his arms, he pressed his lips lingeringly to the Jewish girl's red mouth, kissing the breath out of her body. Suddenly he bit her so viciously that a trickle of blood flowed down her chin and on to her bodice. Once again she looked him in the face and, as she bathed the wound, she muttered:

'You shall pay for this.'

'Oh, I'll pay for it,' he replied with a hard laugh.

Champagne was served at dessert. The major rose to his feet, and in tones in which he would have proposed the health of the Empress Augusta, he exclaimed:

'The ladies!'

A series of toasts followed, toasts that smacked of their drunken gallantry, mingled with obscene jokes, rendered coarser than ever by their ignorance of the language. Each officer in turn sprang to his feet, and made a desperate attempt to be witty and amusing. Too drunk to stand, with vacant gaze and clammy lips, the women welcomed each sally with frantic applause.

Intending, doubtless, to lend to the orgy an atmosphere of gallantry, the captain raised his glass again:

'To our victories over hearts!'

At this Lieutenant Otto, a rough sort of bear from the Black Forest, saturated and inflamed with alcohol, started to his feet:

'To our victories over France!'

Drunk through they were, the women were struck silent, and with a shudder Rachel turned and looked at him:

'I know some Frenchmen before whom you wouldn't

dare say a thing like that.'

The marquis, who still held her on his knee, had drunk himself into a state of great hilarity. He burst out laughing.

'Ha ha ha! Personally I have never seen any Frenchmen. As soon as we come on the scene they take to their heels.'

'Dirty liar!' the girl shouted furiously in his face.

For a moment he fixed her with his light eyes, just as he had done with the portrait of the lady before he had shot at it with his revolver.

'That's all very well, my beauty. But if they had had an ounce of plunk, should we be here? We are their masters,' he added with growing excitement. 'France is ours.'

She jerked herself off his knees and dropped into her chair. The marquis rose to his feet, and holding his glass half-way across the table he repeated:

'France is ours, and the French, and their woods, and their fields, and their houses.'

All the other men were suddenly inflamed with military ardour, with the enthusiasm of brutes. Seizing their glasses they shouted: 'Prussia for ever!' and emptied them at one draught.

The young women dared not protest. They sat cowed and silent. Even Rachel held her peace and did not venture to reply. Then the marquis balanced his newly-filled glass of champagne on Rachel's head, exclaiming:

'And the women of France are ours, too.'

At this Rachel sprang up so fiercely that she upset the glass, which emptied its yellow fluid as if in baptism all over her black hair. Then it fell to the ground and was shattered. Though her lips were trembling, her eyes braved the Prussian officer, who was still laughing. In a voice choked with passion she stammered:

'Oh, that's not true. At any rate that's not true. You will never have the women of France.'

The marquis sat down to give rein to his mirth, and, mimicking the accent of Paris, exclaimed:

'Isn't she funny? Isn't she funny? Then what are you doing here, my pretty dear?'

At first she was too much taken aback to reply. His meaning eluded her, but as soon as she grasped what he said, she burst out in vehement indignation:

'What am I doing here? I? I'm not a woman. I'm only a whore. And that's exactly what you Prussians deserve.'

The words were hardly out of her mouth when the marquis boxed her ears violently. He was raising his hand again in a fury, when she snatched up a small silver dessert knife from the table, and with a gesture so sudden that no one was aware of her intention, she drove it right into the hollow where the neck joins the chest. The word he was uttering was strangled in his throat, and he sat there with his mouth open and a terrible expression on his face.

A shout of horror burst from the whole party, and they all sprang to their feet in consternation. Rachel hurled her chair at the legs of Lieutenant Otto, who measured his length on the floor. Before any one could stop her, she rushed to the window, flung it open, and plunged into the night and the rain.

Two minutes later Mademoiselle Fifi was dead.

At this Fritz and Otto drew their swords to cut down the women, who had thrown themselves on their knees. The major had some difficulty in preventing this massacre. He shut up the four distracted girls in a room with two men to guard them. Then, as if he were disposed his soldiers for battle, he organized the pursuit, never doubting that the fugitive would be recaptured. Urged on by threats, fifty men were scattered all over the park. Two hundred more scoured the woods and searched every house in the valley.

In a moment the table was cleared. It served Mademoiselle Fifi for a bier. Suddenly sobered, the four remaining officers stood rigidly at the windows, peering into the night with the set faces of soldiers on duty. And still the rain poured in torrents. Out of the darkness came a pattering sound, a vague gurgling of water, falling, flowing, dripping, splashing.

All at once a shot rang out, followed by another in the far distance. And during the next four hours more shots were heard, remote or near, with rallying cries and unknown words shouted in gutteral voices, as the men called to one another. In the morning the search parties returned to the château. Two soldiers had been killed and three others wounded by their comrades in the heat and confusion of this noctural hunt.

Rachel had not been found.

A reign of terror ensued for the inhabitants. Their houses

were ransacked; the entire neighbourhood was scoured, searched, patrolled. But the young Jewess seemed to have vanished without leaving a single trace.

The affair was reported to the general, who ordered it to be hushed up, fearing the demoralizing effect of such an example on the army. He visited his displeasure on the major, who in turn punished his subordinates.

The general remarked:

'You do not make war for pleasure, or for the sake of amusing yourself with improper young women.'

In his resentment Count von Falsberg resolved to revenge himself on the village. Seeking a pretext which would justify the utmost serverity, he sent for the priest and ordered him to have the church bell rung at the Marquis von Eyrik's funeral. Contrary to his expectation the priest received his instructions with exemplary docility and deference. And when the body of Mademoiselle Fifi, borne by soldiers, and preceded, followed, and surrounded yet by more soldiers, all carrying loaded rifles, was conveyed from the château to the cemetery, the church bell spoke for the first time. It tolled the funeral knell with a certain blitheness, as if in response to the caress of a friendly hand. It rang again that evening, and the next day, and every succeeding day, chiming away to heart's content. And even during the night it sometimes began to oscillate all by itself and to utter a gentle tinkle through the darkness, as if possessed by a mysterious gaiety and vibrating under some secret influence. The peasants declared that it was bewitched, and no one except the priest and the sacristan ventured near the belfry.

The explanation, however, was simple. An unhappy girl was hiding there, in anguish and solitude, ministered to in secret by those two men. She remained concealed there till the departure of the German troops. Then, one evening, the priest borrowed the baker's wagonette, and himself drove his captive as far as the gates of Rouen. There he kissed her, and she alighted. She made her way back to her old establishment, whose mistress had given her up for dead.

Some time afterwards she was rescued by a man whose patriotism outweighed his prejudices. Loving her first for her noble deed and afterwards for her own sake, he married her and made of her a lady, no less deserving than many another.

Phoenix 60p Paperbacks

History/Biography/Travel
The Empire of Rome A.D. 98–190 *Edward Gibbon*
The Prince *Machiavelli*
The Alan Clark Diaries: Thatcher's Fall *Alan Clark*
Churchill: Embattled Hero *Andrew Roberts*
The French Revolution *E.J. Hobsbawm*
Voyage Around the Horn *Joshua Slocum*
The Great Fire of London *Samuel Pepys*
Utopia *Thomas More*
The Holocaust *Paul Johnson*
Tolstoy and History *Isaiah Berlin*

Science and Philosophy
A Guide to Happiness *Epicurus*
Natural Selection *Charles Darwin*
Science, Mind & Cosmos *John Brockman, ed.*
Zarathustra *Friedrich Nietzsche*
God's Utility Function *Richard Dawkins*
Human Origins *Richard Leakey*
Sophie's World: The Greek Philosophers *Jostein Gaarder*
The Rights of Woman *Mary Wollstonecraft*
The Communist Manifesto *Karl Marx & Friedrich Engels*
Birds of Heaven *Ben Okri*

Fiction
Riot at Misri Mandi *Vikram Seth*
The Time Machine *H. G. Wells*

Love in the Night *F. Scott Fitzgerald*
The Murders in the Rue Morgue *Edgar Allan Poe*
The Necklace *Guy de Maupassant*
You Touched Me *D. H. Lawrence*
The Mabinogion *Anon*
Mowgli's Brothers *Rudyard Kipling*
Shancarrig *Maeve Binchy*
A Voyage to Lilliput *Jonathan Swift*

POETRY
Songs of Innocence and Experience *William Blake*
The Eve of Saint Agnes *John Keats*
High Waving Heather *The Brontes*
Sailing to Byzantium *W. B. Yeats*
I Sing the Body Electric *Walt Whitman*
The Ancient Mariner *Samuel Taylor Coleridge*
Intimations of Immortality *William Wordsworth*
Palgrave's Golden Treasury of Love Poems *Francis Palgrave*
Goblin Market *Christina Rossetti*
Fern Hill *Dylan Thomas*

LITERATURE OF PASSION
Don Juan *Lord Byron*
From Bed to Bed *Catullus*
Satyricon *Petronius*
Love Poems *John Donne*
Portrait of a Marriage *Nigel Nicolson*
The Ballad of Reading Gaol *Oscar Wilde*
Love Sonnets *William Shakespeare*
Fanny Hill *John Cleland*
The Sexual Labyrinth (for women) *Alina Reyes*
Close Encounters (for men) *Alina Reyes*